CITY COLLEGE NORWICH
LIBRARY SERVICES

THE USBORNE SOCCER SCHOOL

GOALKEEPING

Jonathan Sheikh-Miller

Designed by Neil Francis

Edited by Felicity Brooks • Managing Designer [illegible] Wright

Photographs by Chris [illegible]

Library photographs: Action Images and [illegible]
Soccer boots courtesy of Reebok UK

Illustrations by Bob Bond

Consultants: John Shiels,
Bobby Charlton International Soccer Schools Ltd.;
Peter Bonetti, Chelsea and England

With special thanks to players Osman Afzal, Sajid Aziz, Leanne Davis, Lindsey Jamieson, Matthew Rea, Ciaran Simpson, Mark Davis, David [illegible], and to their coaches, Dave Benson and Gavin Rhodes.

DTP by John Russell

KT-418-718

NORWICH CITY COLLEGE LIBRARY
Stock No. 226101
Class 796.334 SHE
Cat. SSA Proc. 3WKL B/P

CONTENTS

2 Goalkeeping basics
4 Ready to save
6 Good handling
8 Shots near the keeper
10 Diving saves
12 Positioning
14 One-on-ones
16 Handling crosses
18 Throwing
20 Kicking
22 Helping the defence
24 Corners and throw-ins
26 Free kicks and penalties
28 Recovery save practice
30 Pre-match preparation
32 Index

GOALKEEPING BASICS

The goalkeeper is one of the most important players in a soccer team. All successful teams have a very good goalkeeper as well as a strong defence. A keeper's main job is to protect the goal, but he also helps organize the defence, and his kicks and throws can lead to sudden or gradual attacks. This book shows you how to develop the skills and qualities you need to be a good keeper.

WHAT MAKES A GOOD KEEPER?

Decisiveness – you need to be able to think quickly every time there is an attack on your goal (see page 14).

Agility – you will often have to jump, fall and dive as you try to stop a shot at goal (see page 10).

Courage – you will have to dive and jump in crowded penalty areas with many legs, elbows and boots around you (see page 14).

A cool head – if you make a mistake or are faced with a high pressure situation, you need to be able to keep calm and focus on the game (see page 15).

You can find out how to do acrobatic diving saves, like this one, on page 10.

Good co-ordination – sometimes you will need to change direction very quickly and make fast reflex saves (see page 29).

Good communication – your defence will want to hear clear instructions at 'set piece plays' (see pages 22 and 24).

Positional sense – you will need to be able to vary your position in the goal to make it harder for attackers to shoot (see page 12).

STAR KEEPER

Many soccer experts believe that Danish keeper Peter Schmeichel has played a big part in Manchester United's success.

GOALKEEPING LAWS

There are a number of laws of the game which you will need to know about as a keeper. Soccer laws can change quite often, so you will need to keep up to date with them. Breaking a law is 'foul play' and a free kick may be given against you.

★ When you have the ball in your hands, you can only take up to four paces before you must release it.

★ After you have taken hold of the ball, you must get it out to your team-mates in no more than five or six seconds.

★ You can only handle the ball inside your own penalty area. If you come out of the area, use your feet or head when you touch the ball. Breaking this law is very serious, and you might get sent off.

★ If a team-mate passes the ball back to you, or throws a throw-in directly to you, you cannot use your hands to control the ball. You can handle headers and passes that come off the chest or thigh.

USEFUL KICKING TERMS

This book uses a number of special terms to describe the parts of the foot and the stages in kicking a ball.

*Your **backswing** is when you swing your leg back before you kick the ball.*

*Your **follow-through** is when you swing your leg up after kicking the ball.*

*The **inside** of your foot stretches from your big toe back to your ankle.*

*Your **instep** is the flat area over your laces, but not including your toes.*

PARTS OF THE PITCH

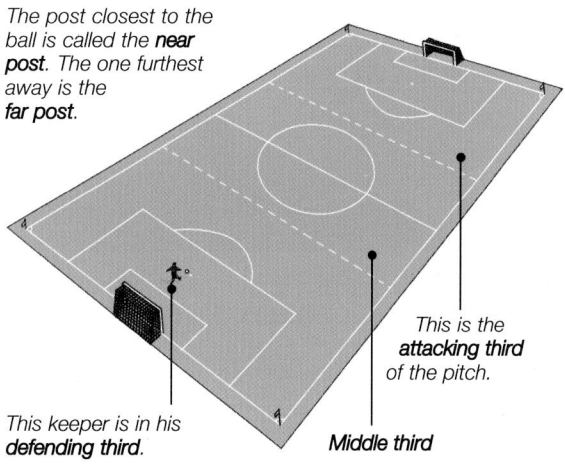

You will spend most of your time in your team's defending third of the pitch. When your team is attacking, then play is in your attacking third. The area in-between is called the middle third.

READY TO SAVE

When you think you've got what it takes to be a goalkeeper, then the next step is to get hold of the right equipment and learn the vital goalkeeping skills of quick movement around the goal area and reliable handling of the ball.

GOALKEEPER'S STANCE

When you're waiting to make a save, you should stand in a set position. This allows you to react quickly to attacks on the goal.

Keep your head still and your eyes on the ball.

This is the typical stance used by goalkeepers. It shows you are alert and ready.

Try to lean forwards slightly so you are ready to make quick and sudden falls or jumps.

Your hands should be at around waist height with palms facing outwards.

Your legs should be slightly bent, and about a shoulder width apart.

Your weight should be equally balanced on the balls of your feet.

WHAT TO WEAR

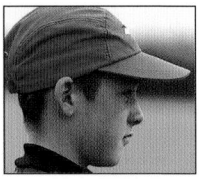

A cap or visor keeps the sun out of your eyes when dealing with high balls.

Wear loose, comfortable clothes. Diving and bending isn't easy in tight clothes.

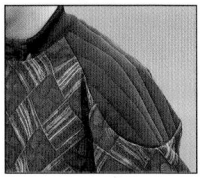

A shirt with padded elbows and shoulders helps to protect you when you dive.

Gloves with latex palms help to give you much more grip on the ball.

On hard ground, wear tracksuit bottoms to protect your knees.

MOVING AROUND THE GOAL AREA

When you are comfortable with the keeper's stance, you can practise moving quickly around the goal area. If you can move well, catches are much easier to take, as you get more of your body behind the ball. Try moving in the set position, taking small sideways steps. Don't cross your feet as it can slow you down. Then ask a team-mate to move backwards and forwards across the penalty area. Try to mirror his movements.

Try to mirror your team-mate's movements.

Don't open your legs too wide.

THE W SHAPE

For shots or headers that come towards you at chest or head height, the most effective catching technique is the W shape. The palms of your hands face outwards and your index fingers and thumbs form a 'W' around the back of the ball. Your fingers need to be spread wide and thumbs should be about an inch or two (2-5cm) apart.

As the shot approaches, you need to keep your eyes on the ball. If you look away from the ball, this could mean a dropped catch and a rebound to an opponent.

Keep your hands well in front of your body, so you can watch the ball as you catch it.

Make sure your fingers are relaxed and flexible so that they absorb the impact of a shot. The ball might bounce out of rigid, tense hands.

This is how your hands should look when you catch using the W shape.

CATCHING AND MOVING

This game will help you to practise combining your sideways movement in the set position with taking catches at chest or head height.

Lay out a zigzag pattern of sports markers on a pitch with a gap of about 2m (6ft) between each one. Weave through the markers, staying in the set stance.

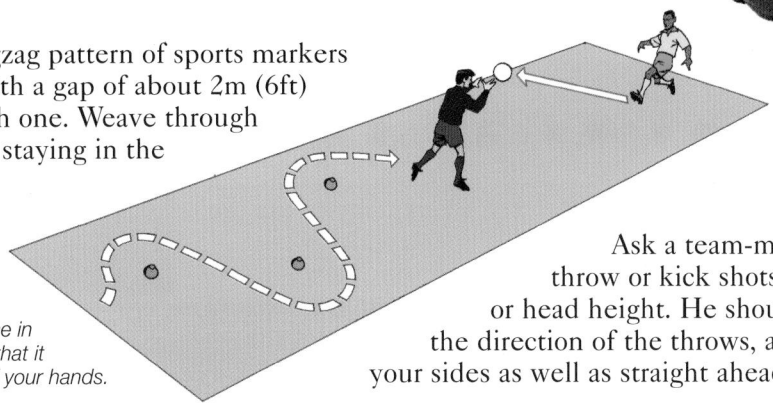

After you catch, bring the ball close in to your body, so that it cannot slip out of your hands.

Ask a team-mate to throw or kick shots at chest or head height. He should vary the direction of the throws, aiming to your sides as well as straight ahead.

GOOD HANDLING

The W shape is a useful basic catching technique, but because the ball comes at many different heights and angles, you also need to get to know other ways of handling it. No matter where the ball is coming from, good footwork will make handling a lot easier.

CRADLING THE BALL

Scooping the ball into your body is the best method to use with balls that come at waist or stomach height. It is a very safe way of catching and some keepers use the scoop with chest high balls too.

Cradle the ball with your hands and arms.

As the ball comes into contact with your chest or stomach, wrap your hands and forearms around the back of the ball. Your body will cushion the impact of a shot. Try not to step back as you catch.

As the shot arrives, angle your hands downwards, giving the ball a clear path to travel into your body.

USEFUL TIPS

★ Always try to lean into a shot. This makes it much easier to scoop the ball into your body.

★ You may need to take a small jump to get your upper body behind a slightly higher shot.

★ It's very risky to use the W shape with a waist high shot, as you can't get your eyes behind the flight of the incoming ball.

STAR SCOOP

This Derby County keeper makes a good scoop while under pressure in an English Premier League game.

THE BARRIER POSITION

The barrier is the safer of the two methods you can use for ground level shots. It takes time to get down into this position, so it's best to use the barrier when you have a clear view of the ball or can see the shot early.

Place one knee on the ground, with your leg in the position shown in the picture. Put the foot of your other leg lengthwise alongside it, so that you make a long barrier.

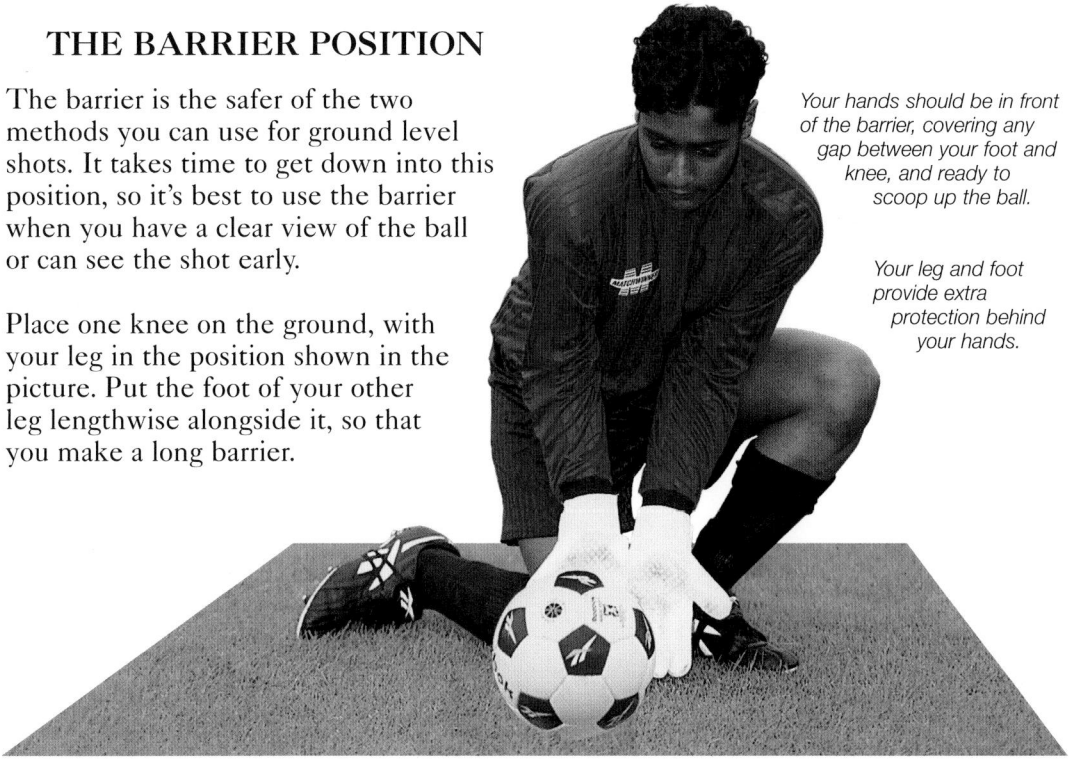

Your hands should be in front of the barrier, covering any gap between your foot and knee, and ready to scoop up the ball.

Your leg and foot provide extra protection behind your hands.

THE BENDING SCOOP

It isn't easy to get into the safer barrier position quickly, so with faster ground shots it's better to use the bending scoop. This position relies upon good footwork and close attention to the movement of the ball.

As the shot approaches, bring your feet close together. Then bend down and scoop the ball into your hands.

It's risky to use this method on uneven playing surfaces and in bad weather conditions. An unexpected deflection of the ball can cause serious problems.

HIGH AND LOW SHOT PRACTICE

This game will help you practise catching shots aimed at different heights. You will need two other players.

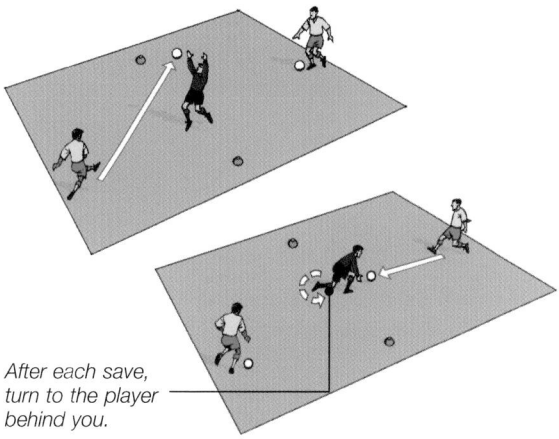

After each save, turn to the player behind you.

Mark out a goal 3m (10ft) wide, and place two team-mates 5m (16ft) away on either side of it, each with a ball. One player provides chest and head high shots, the other player hits ground shots. This is a tiring drill, so swap around regularly.

SHOTS NEAR THE KEEPER

Some shots come too quickly for you to have time to do a kneeling or bending save. When you need to get down to the ball as fast as possible, falling to the ground is the best solution. Practising falling saves will help you get ready to try diving saves later on.

THE COLLAPSING SAVE

When a ball is aimed close to you, there is no need to dive for it. What you should do instead is move quickly out of the set stance and collapse onto the shot. When you do a collapsing save, swing your legs to one side and drop down to the ball hands first. Your body will act as a barrier behind your hands. Try not to land on your elbows (see page 10).

Notice how the goalkeeper above is already looking to position his hands behind the ball. Although he has begun to swing his legs to one side, the top half of his body is steady and focused on the ball.

The keeper puts both hands on the ball. One hand wraps around the back of the ball, while the other is on top.

The wrapping hand acts as a barrier. The hand on top grips the ball to his body.

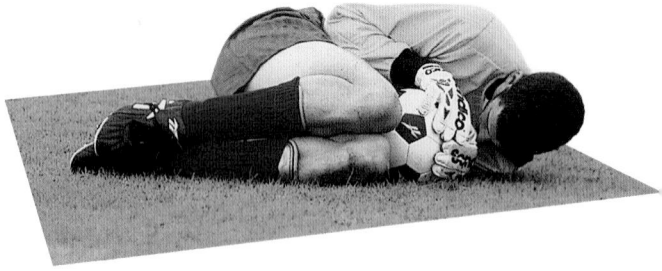

Once the shot has been stopped, the keeper pulls the ball in close to his chest. He then curls himself around the ball to help protect his body in a crowded goal area.

COLLAPSING TIPS

★ You should practise collapsing saves regularly, because many keepers find them very difficult to do.

★ Don't overdo your collapsing movement. It shouldn't involve any jumping or acrobatic leaps.

★ The ball will be moving fast, so get your hands down in time, otherwise the ball will squeeze under your body.

This keeper didn't move fast enough.

SAVING WITH YOUR FEET

When a shot is fired in from very close range, you will need to react fast to make a save. If you don't have time to get your hands to the ball, you'll have to save with your feet and legs.

As the ball approaches, keep your weight well balanced and turn your feet outwards. Watch the ball very closely and try to use your legs as a barrier.

Saving with your feet should only be attempted as a final option. This type of save is instinctive and you have no control over where the ball rebounds to.

Saving with your feet is a good reflex reaction when a shot comes at you through a crowd of players (see page 28).

HANDS AND FEET PRACTICE

Mark out a goal about 4m (13ft) wide within the goal area. Place two more markers the same distance apart about 3m (10ft) out from goal. Do the same again about 6m (20ft) out.

Ask a team-mate to stand on a line level with either set of markers and take shots at goal. Swap with your team-mate when you feel tired. Use your hands to save whenever possible.

Practise collapsing saves for longer shots.

Save with your feet and legs for closer, faster shots.

PREPARING FOR DIVING SAVES

Diving saves involve a lot of falling on the ground. Here are two games to give you more practice in this, before you learn how to dive. It's best to practise with another keeper, who can also get used to falling.

1. Your team-mate rolls the ball through your legs. Turn around quickly and fall on the ball before it is out of your reach.

2. Your team-mate throws balls a metre (3ft) either side of you. Crouch down to catch them, falling on your side as you catch.

DIVING SAVES

When attackers fire wider shots at goal, you'll need to attempt a diving save. Successful acrobatic diving saves give goalkeepers a lot of satisfaction and can make the difference between winning or losing a match. However, there is much more to a diving save than simply leaping into the air. The right jumping and landing techniques are essential.

A DIVING CATCH

When you spot the 'flight', or direction, of the ball, take a few quick sideways paces to reduce your diving distance. Stay focused on the ball in the set stance.

Just before you are about to dive, quickly transfer your weight onto the foot nearest the incoming ball. Push down hard on this foot and then begin to leap up.

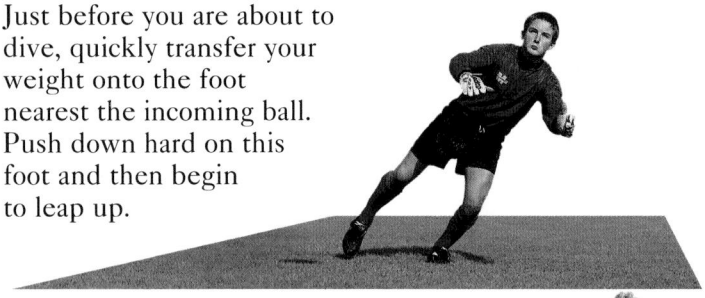

Try to get as much thrust or 'spring' from your leg as possible. As you leap up, keep your eyes on the ball and dive slightly forwards to attack the shot.

Use the W shape catching technique, letting your hands absorb the power of the shot. Grasp the ball tightly so that it doesn't bounce out of your hands when you land.

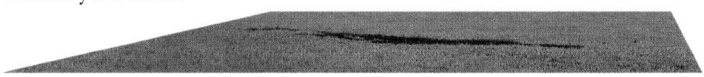

A SAFE LANDING

It's vital to learn a safe landing technique. When you hit the ground, try to land on your side, as this is a well cushioned part of the body. Don't come down on your elbows or your stomach.

Keep your body relaxed as you land.

If you are playing on an artificial surface or on hard ground, tracksuit bottoms can help prevent painful grazes to the knees.

THE CAT

Many diving saves require impressive agility and suppleness.

In the 1960s and '70s, Peter Bonetti of Chelsea and England became known as 'The Cat', because of his quick reflexes and diving technique.

TIPPING THE BALL

You should aim to catch most diving saves, but if a shot is too powerful or too well-placed to catch, you should still try to get a touch on the ball as it goes by.

A slight deflection, or tip, of the ball can be enough to push it off target. When the shot touches your hand, make sure your palm is open and your fingers are spread wide. Try to push or flick the ball away.

Keeping your palm open makes a bigger target for the ball to hit.

Use only one hand to deflect the ball.

When you deflect the ball away, try to tip it over the bar or around the post.

PLAY SAFE

If you push the ball straight out in front, you could give it to an opposing striker.

The safest option is putting it out of play for a corner. You can tip the ball with either hand as you dive, but try to use the hand nearest the ball. Use your upper hand for tipping over the bar, and your lower hand for pushing the ball around the post.

DIVING TIPS

★ It is better to use swift footwork to get closer to the ball and make an easier save than to attempt a difficult diving save.

★ All keepers have a favourite diving side but you should be a strong diver on both sides. Spend extra time building up your weaker spring.

IMPROVING YOUR DIVES

This game helps you get used to the hard impact with the ground that follows a diving save. It can also strengthen your spring off the ground. Ask a team-mate or another keeper to shoot or throw the ball just inside either post of a full size goal. Stand in the middle of the goal before each shot and as the ball approaches, leap up off the foot nearest the ball. Swap around after four or five diving saves.

Try to catch every shot. Only tip the ball away if you have to.

Be careful that you don't collide with the posts. Always watch your position.

POSITIONING

In goalkeeping, good positional sense is as important as sound handling skills, especially when the ball is in the defending third of the pitch. Good positioning involves skilful footwork and getting your body behind the ball. This makes a lot of saves easier for you and also makes shooting at goal harder for your opponents.

GETTING IN LINE

Keepers like to position themselves somewhere on an imaginary line between the ball and the centre of the goal. This is known as being in line with play.

This keeper is in line with play and so as a shot comes in, he can get his body behind the ball and make a simple save.

Here the keeper hasn't managed to keep in line with play. As a shot approaches, he is at full stretch and has to make a much more difficult save.

NARROWING THE ANGLE

Good keepers not only need to be in line but off their goal-line too. By coming off the goal-line, keepers reduce the view of the goal for attackers and 'narrow' the shooting angle. Shots become much easier for the keeper to reach.

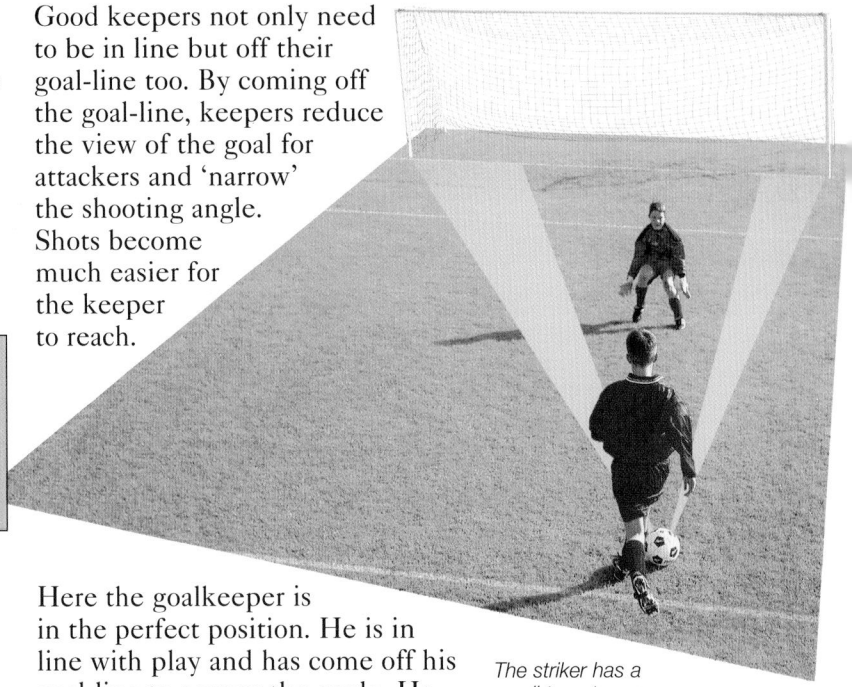

The striker has a small target area.

Here the goalkeeper is in the perfect position. He is in line with play and has come off his goal-line to narrow the angle. He can handle shots to his left or right.

Here the keeper is in real trouble. He is out of position and has left both sides of the goal wide open. He has failed to narrow the angle, giving the striker the chance to close in on goal.

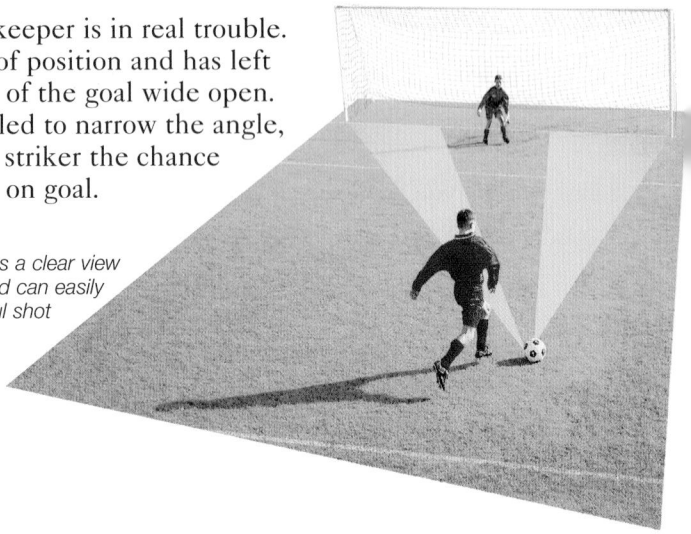

This striker has a clear view of the goal and can easily aim a powerful shot either side of the keeper.

IN THE DEFENDING THIRD

You should always be in line when the ball is in your defending third of the pitch. How far off your goal-line you should be depends on where play is taking place, and if you think that your goal area is under threat of attack from a sudden shot or cross.

Here, the ball is well away from goal. The shooting angle is difficult and the goal is well covered, so there is no direct threat. The keeper can be a little way off his line, as he has time to adjust his position.

Here, the attack is inside the penalty area and the striker will soon be in a position to shoot. The keeper must not be too far off his goal-line as he is directly involved in play. He must be well in line with the ball.

THE CHIP SHOT

A keeper should be well off his line and in touch with play when the opposition are on the attack, but he mustn't rush out too fast.

This keeper is rushing out to narrow the angle.

The striker lobs the ball into the unguarded goal.

If a striker is nearing the goal and sees the keeper off his line, he may try to lob, or chip, the ball over his head (see page 28).

RECOVERING POSITION

You must always be ready to change your position quickly. A sudden sideways pass near or inside the penalty area will leave you well out of line. You need to get in line again fast, before an attacker can shoot into the open space.

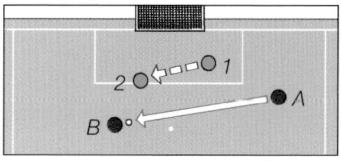

Here, player A passes to player B. The keeper should move from position 1, where he was covering player A, to position 2 to line up against player B. By making a direct diagonal movement, he will get into position sooner.

THE ANGLES GAME

This game helps you practise getting in line with play and narrowing shooting angles. Ask two team-mates, each with a ball, to stand on either side of the penalty area about 14m (46ft) out from goal.

Get into line, shout 'ready' and then save from player A.

Do the same with player B. A and B should vary their positions before each shot.

ONE-ON-ONES

A defensive mistake or a great pass can lead to a striker being through on goal, with only the keeper to beat. These 'one-on-one' situations are a real test of technique and temperament for any goalkeeper.

FORCING THE ATTACKER WIDE

You need to position yourself well and react quickly and positively if you are to have any chance of stopping an attacker's run on goal. Don't commit yourself too early to rushing out, but try to narrow the shooting angle and force the attacker wide, away from goal. This will make it more difficult for him to shoot and will give defenders a chance to get back and support you. Be ready for a sudden shot.

1. As the striker is running onto a pass but has not yet touched the ball, get quickly off your line and narrow the shooting angle.

2. Once the striker has the ball, slow down, and watch out for a shot. Get into the set stance and block the route to goal.

3. As the striker tries to take the ball around you, stay in line and force him wide. It is now much harder for him to score.

DIVING AT AN ATTACKER'S FEET

When a striker attempts to dribble the ball around you, try to gain possession by diving at the player's feet.

This type of save is difficult and you need a lot of courage and a cool head. Only dive if you feel sure you will win possession. Be positive and attack the ball.

The best time to make your move is when the ball is slightly ahead of the attacker and not totally under control.

Go in hands first for the ball. By keeping them in front of your face, you help to protect your head.

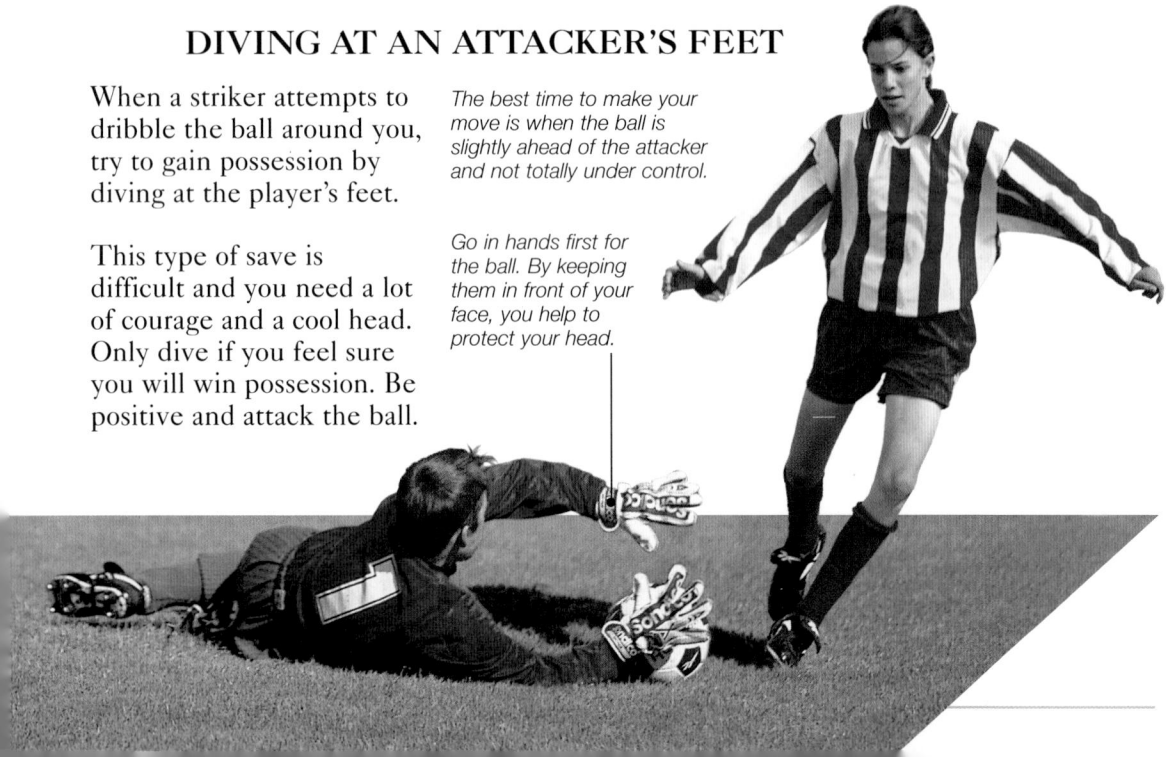

SPREADING YOURSELF

As you go down to save at an attacker's feet, try to 'spread yourself' on the ground, making a long barrier between the ball and the goal. This will also help narrow the angle.

Get down low, trying not to leave any gaps between your body and the ground. Once you have claimed the ball, wrap your body around it for extra security.

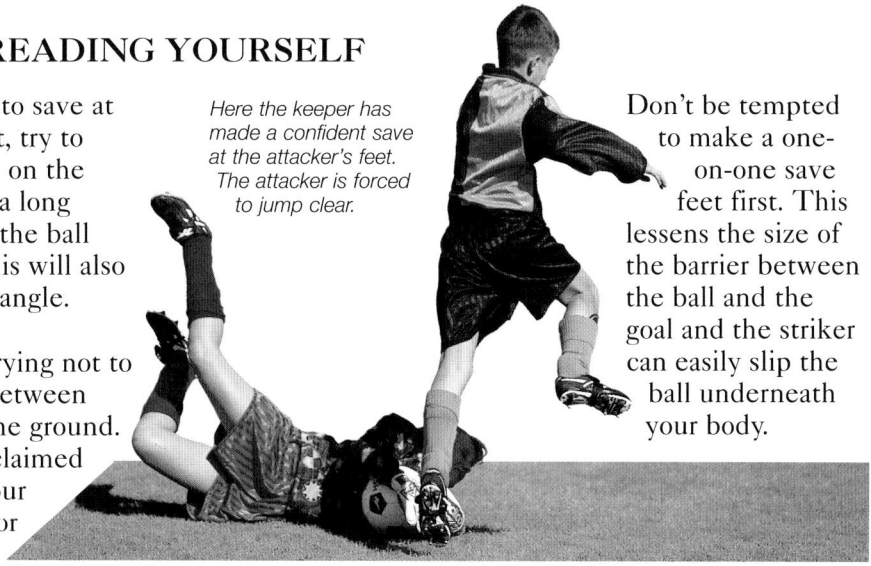

Here the keeper has made a confident save at the attacker's feet. The attacker is forced to jump clear.

Don't be tempted to make a one-on-one save feet first. This lessens the size of the barrier between the ball and the goal and the striker can easily slip the ball underneath your body.

SPREADING PRACTICE

This drill helps you to judge the moment when to dive at an attacker's feet. Mark out a pitch about 10m (33ft) square. Ask two team-mates to keep possession of the ball as you move about in the set stance, diving at their feet. Don't be tempted to save feet first.

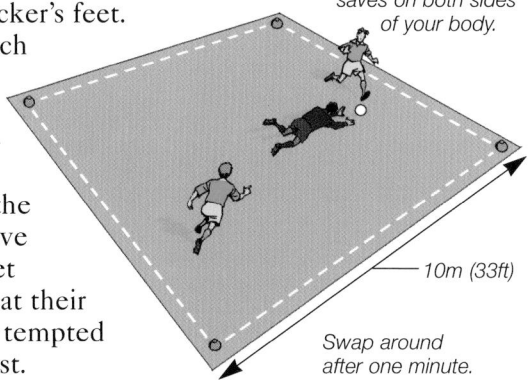

This game lets you practise spreading saves on both sides of your body.

Swap around after one minute.

STAYING COOL

One-on-ones are very pressurized situations. You should try to stay calm and not make any rash decisions. Remember that the striker is under more pressure than you are. He is expected to score and has to decide very quickly how to get the ball past you, and into the net.

If you know your opponent has one weaker shooting foot, force him to take the ball on that side.

Looking big and confident can unsettle a striker – so don't crouch down too far in your stance. Waving your hands or arms around quickly can also affect a striker's concentration.

STAR BLOCK

Here Coventry City goalkeeper Steve Ogrizovic shows a lot of courage and prevents an almost certain goal, by making an impressive spreading save.

He bravely dives at the feet of Newcastle United's Georgian international midfielder Temur Ketsbaia and wins possession of the ball.

HANDLING CROSSES

Many goals come from high crosses aimed deep into the penalty area. Every cross is different, and you need to decide whether to come for a cross or leave it for your defence to clear. Catch a cross if you can, but punch or tip if you have to. If you decide to deal with a cross, be positive and go for the ball.

POSITIONING FOR CROSSES

Where you stand for a cross depends on where the crosser is. Half turn your body towards the crosser so that you can watch movements in the area as well as the ball.

Here, the ball is near the wing and a long way out from goal. The keeper is positioned in the centre of the goal so that he won't be left stranded by a cross over his head. Moving backwards and catching a ball under pressure isn't easy.

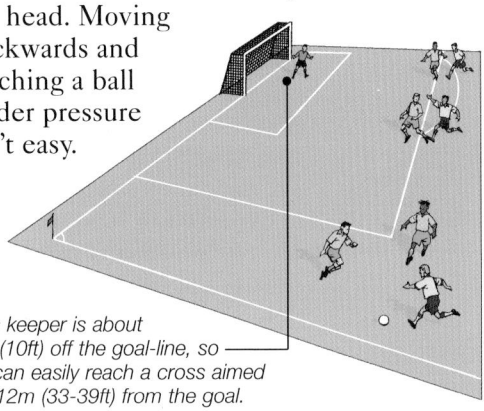

This keeper is about 3m (10ft) off the goal-line, so he can easily reach a cross aimed 10-12m (33-39ft) from the goal.

Play has now moved away from the wing and well into the attacking third of the pitch. The keeper is moving closer to the near post to narrow the angle. He must still be alert to the chance of a far post cross.

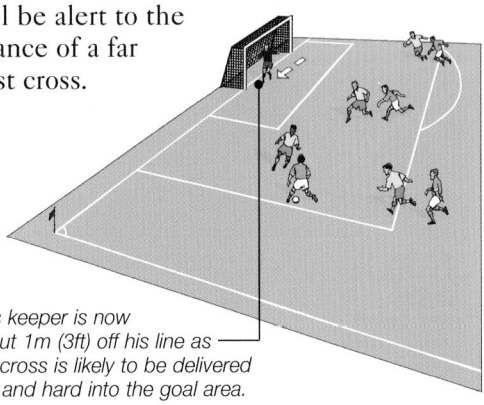

This keeper is now about 1m (3ft) off his line as the cross is likely to be delivered low and hard into the goal area.

A CLEAN CATCH

You need good communication with your defence (see page 22) when dealing with a cross. If you decide you can reach an incoming cross and can make a clean catch without other players getting in your way, then clearly shout 'Keeper's ball!' as you take a running jump for it.

Jump off one leg and catch the ball about 30cm (1ft) in front of your face, using the W shape.

Lift up the leg nearest to the opposition to protect your lower body against challenges.

As you jump, turn sideways on to the opposition and face the ball. Try to catch a cross when the ball is at its highest point. This makes it harder for strikers to get up and reach the ball. When you have dealt with a cross, be ready to make a quick throw (see page 18) to start an attack.

TWO-HANDED PUNCHES

Sometimes other players can get in your way or put you under so much pressure that you are unable to catch the ball. In this case, try to punch it away instead. A good punched clearance needs height and distance to give you enough time to recover your position if the ball goes straight to an opponent.

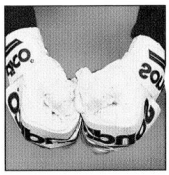

This is how you clench your fists for a two-handed punch.

Aim for the lower half of the ball.

Take a running jump at the ball and shout 'Keeper's ball!' To get maximum power in your punches you need to use two clenched fists. This also offers a larger surface area for the ball to hit. Keep your fists together and strike the ball firmly with the part of your hands between the knuckles and the finger joints.

ONE-HANDED PUNCHES

If you can't get two hands to the ball, you may have to use a less powerful one-handed punch.

One-handed punches are quite difficult to do because you only have a small punching surface.

When the ball is drifting over your head, and you have to move backwards quickly, a one-handed punch will strike the ball out of danger towards the opposite wing.

TIPPING

If an inswinging cross is aimed deep into the goal area and you are under a lot of pressure, you could try tipping the ball over the bar for a corner (see page 11).

Use the hand which is furthest from the goal, to get a much bigger swing at the ball.

When you tip the ball out for a corner, you are giving possession straight back to the opposition. A catch or strong punch is safer.

CROSSES GAME

This game should get you used to handling under pressure and timing your jumps. Stand in the centre of a goal and ask two team-mates, each with a ball, to supply crosses from the wings.

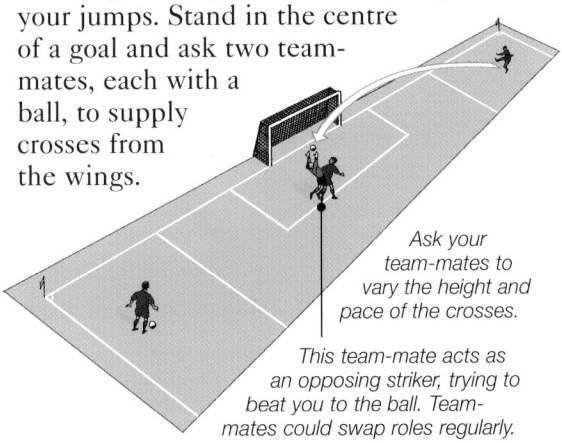

Ask your team-mates to vary the height and pace of the crosses.

This team-mate acts as an opposing striker, trying to beat you to the ball. Team-mates could swap roles regularly.

THROWING

Accurate and reliable distribution of the ball to your team-mates is an essential skill for a keeper. Well placed throws or kicks can lead to dangerous attacks on your opposition's goal. There are three main types of throw and each can be effective in opening up space for an unmarked team-mate.

THE UNDERARM ROLL

You use the underarm roll when you are aiming for a team-mate no more than 8m (26ft) away. As he will be positioned near the goal, use this throw when no opponents are close by. Don't use this type of throw on muddy pitches, as the ball might get stuck.

For an underarm throw, start by swinging your throwing arm back.

Get down quite low. Your front foot should point in the direction of the throw.

Swing your throwing arm forwards, releasing the ball at the last moment.

Keep the ball low, rolling it along the ground.

THE JAVELIN THROW

Use the javelin throw to cover distances of up to 15m (49ft). Your target might be a team-mate who has moved into space on the wing or who has dropped back from midfield. Javelin throws should be delivered low and fast to their target, so try not to throw the ball too high in the air.

Bend your knees slightly to help keep the ball low as you release it.

Bend your throwing arm back and bring the ball up level with your shoulder. Aim your non-throwing arm at the target and point your front foot in the same direction.

Swing your throwing arm forwards quickly and release the ball. Flicking your wrist will help keep the ball low. For extra distance on your throw, follow through powerfully.

THE OVERARM THROW

Use the overarm throw to cover distances of 15m (49ft) or more. When your technique is well developed, the overarm throw can travel nearly as far as a kick. This throw is very good for getting the ball upfield quickly once an opposition attack has broken down. A fast, well placed throw can leave opponents badly out of position and can turn defence into attack.

Bring your throwing arm back behind your body. Keep it straight. Point your non-throwing arm and your front foot at the target.

Swing your throwing arm powerfully upwards and over your shoulder.

Transfer your weight onto your front foot. To get height on the throw, release the ball when your arm is at its highest point.

WHEN TO THROW

★ Use a throw after cutting out a cross. You can change the direction of play while opponents are still in your defending third.

★ If the opposing team has a tall defence, low throws are a lot better than high kicks for keeping possession.

★ When you are playing in a strong wind, use throws rather than kicks, as they are easier to direct and control.

★ Stick to throwing if you are not a strong kicker. Good throws are better than weak kicks.

WHERE TO THROW

Most throws should be aimed towards the sides of the pitch, where a team-mate may be able to find some space to run into.

A throw aimed into the crowded centre of the pitch will be difficult to control and could be easily intercepted. As most throws travel quite low through the air, you shouldn't try to throw over the heads of opponents.

THROWING GAME

Ask two keepers to help you with this game so you can all practise your throwing skills. Form a triangle, 6m (20ft) apart, and roll the ball underarm to each other first.

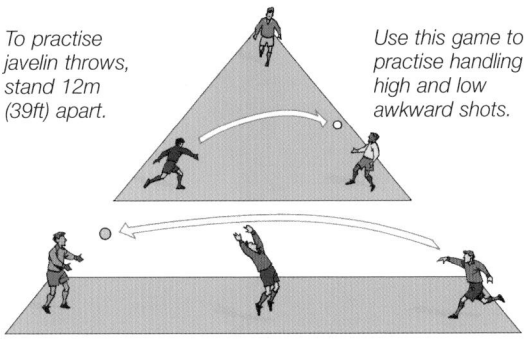

For overarm practice, two throwers stand about 15m (49ft) apart. The other keeper stands in the middle and tries to intercept the throws.

KICKING

Place kicks, volleys and half-volleys give you an opportunity to send the ball a long way upfield, changing defence into attack. Keepers need to be strong accurate kickers, so practise regularly.

THE PLACE KICK

A place kick is a kick taken when the ball is stationary, such as a goal kick or free kick. Long, powerful place kicks help ease pressure on your defence. If your kicks don't travel very far, make sure they are accurate.

Take an angled run-up and put your non-kicking foot to the side of the ball. Your kicking foot swings forwards quickly.

As you kick, lean back slightly and keep your eyes fixed on the ball.

Strike the lower half of the ball with your instep. Follow through powerfully.

THE VOLLEY

To do a volley, you drop the ball from your hands and kick it before it hits the ground. When you are holding the ball, you can take four steps as a run-up before you kick (see page 3). The higher you aim a volley, the longer it will take to reach its target.

As you run, hold the ball in front of you at waist height. Take a good backswing as the ball drops.

Place your non-kicking leg behind the ball. Leaning back slightly will help to get lift on the kick.

Keeping your head steady, kick the bottom of the ball with your instep. Follow-through smoothly.

THE HALF-VOLLEY

When you do a half-volley, the ball bounces once before you kick it. Use half-volleys in windy conditions, as they do not travel as high through the air as volleys. It's risky to try them on muddy or uneven pitches.

Drop the ball from about waist height. It should land just in front of your non-kicking foot.

As the ball bounces, swing your kicking leg forwards, leaning back as you kick.

Watching the ball carefully, strike the bottom half of it with your instep.

WHICH KICK TO CHOOSE

Think carefully about what type of kick to use and don't take any chances. Aim all place kicks to the sides of the pitch, and never kick across the penalty area. Only kick over your opponents' heads with high volleys or half-volleys.

If you are a strong kicker, you might be able to reach the attacking third with a powerful volley.

Half-volleys travel more quickly than volleys and so are good for starting fast, unexpected attacks.

Place kicks aimed to the sides of the pitch are safer and might find team-mates in space.

If your strikers are not good at heading the ball, a short kick to a defender is better than a kick upfield.

TARGET PRACTICE

You will need five or six balls for this game which will improve the accuracy and distance of your kicks. Ask another keeper to help you. Take turns at kicking and retrieving the balls.

For place kicks, kick alternately from either corner of the goal area, aiming inside two markers 6m (20ft) apart on the halfway line.

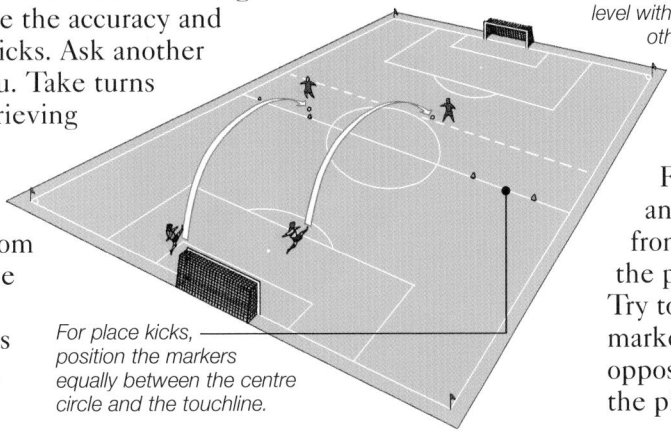

For volleys, position markers level with the circle in the other half of the pitch.

For place kicks, position the markers equally between the centre circle and the touchline.

For half-volleys and volleys, kick from the edge of the penalty area. Try to clear the markers in the opposition's half of the pitch.

HELPING THE DEFENCE

Although as a keeper you have your own important job to do, you should remember that you are part of the defensive unit. A good keeper will communicate with his team-mates and be on-hand to receive back passes and cut out through balls.

TALKING TO YOUR DEFENCE

From the goal area, you have a good view of the pitch and can see how play is developing. This allows you to advise your defenders about what they should do and warn them about possible dangers. You should shout clear, short instructions. Decide with your team-mates before a game what you will shout in different situations. There are several well-known, regular shouts.

'Keeper's ball!' *– shout this to claim possession in any situation, and especially for crosses (see page 16).*

'Peter, pick him up!' *– tells a specific team-mate to mark an opponent who is unmarked.*

'Push up!' *– gets your defence to move upfield, possibly catching opponents offside (see page 23).*

'Time!' *– tells a team-mate with the ball that no opposing players are near enough to challenge him.*

'Played!' *– congratulates a team-mate for some good play. It's good to encourage your team-mates.*

'Man on!' *– warns a team-mate with the ball who is unaware that an opponent is about to tackle him.*

KEEPING UP WITH PLAY

Try to stay in line with play even when the ball is not in your defending third. If you are always in touch with the game, you might be able to offer some support to your team-mates in tricky situations.

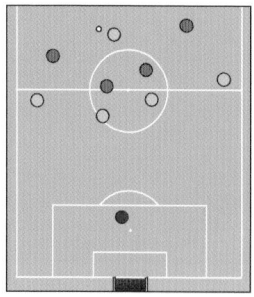

Here play is in the attacking third. The keeper is on the edge of the penalty area, ready to deal with long clearances and through balls.

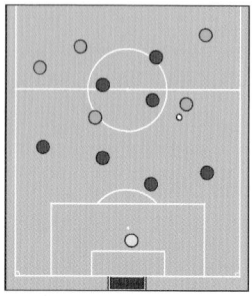

Play is now in the middle third and the keeper has moved back slightly. He can cut out through balls or long-range shots as well as receive back passes.

PLAYING AS A SWEEPER

A good keeper will be ready to act as a defensive 'outfield' player when needed. All players except the keeper are known as outfield players as they are able to move freely about the pitch.

If a team-mate wants to pass the ball back to you, stand a few metres back from him, in case he overhits or misdirects the pass.

Be ready to take on the role of 'sweeper', a spare man at the back of the defence. You can clear up any loose balls and can be on-hand to receive back passes from defenders.

When you receive a back pass, remember that you can only use your hands with headers, not with passes from feet.

THE OFFSIDE RULE

All keepers need to know about the offside rule. You can often stop dangerous attacks by catching opposing attackers offside. Your team is then awarded an indirect free kick.

A player is offside when, just as a pass is made to him, there are less than two opponents between him and the goal. No player can be offside in his own half or if he receives the ball directly from a corner, throw-in or goal kick. Asking your defence to push up to catch strikers offside is risky. If an attacker gets past a defender who has pushed up, he is through on goal.

CLEARANCE KICKS

You will sometimes be in position to intercept dangerous through balls with a powerful one-touch clearance which aims to force the ball well upfield or out of play.

Accuracy is not so important with these kicks, but you must react quickly and kick powerfully while under pressure. Only come out of your area if you are sure you will get to the ball first.

Try to make good, strong contact with the ball for a powerful clearance kick.

CORNERS AND THROW-INS

Corners and throw-ins in your defending third give your opponents the chance to use a 'dead', or stationary, ball to carry out some pre-planned moves, called 'set piece plays'. The fact that no player can be offside if he receives the ball directly from a throw-in or corner makes these moves very dangerous.

ORGANIZING CORNER DEFENCE

As keeper, you are responsible for making sure that your defenders are in a good position and that no opposing attackers are unmarked. Most players in your team will have a particular job to do at a corner, whether marking opposing players or covering different parts of the penalty area. Shout clear instructions to your team-mates and take charge of the situation, making quick, confident decisions.

One or two players should cover the far post and the area in front of it.

One player should guard the area around the near post, with another player nearby to cover a very short corner.

Other players should mark opponents who have come forward for the corner.

You should stand in the centre of the goal, about 1m (3ft) off your line, so you can deal with a near or far post delivery.

One defender should stand on the edge of the goal area to give the keeper extra support.

No defender can come any nearer than 9m (30ft) to the corner taker.

THE NEAR POST MOVE

One of the most dangerous and commonly used set piece plays at a corner is the three touch move which involves an inswinging corner to the near post.

The aim of this move is to get the ball into the goal using just three touches. An attacker swings the corner in to the near post where a tall opponent tries to flick on a header towards the far post. Another player tries to get in front of his marker to meet the flick-on with a header or shot.

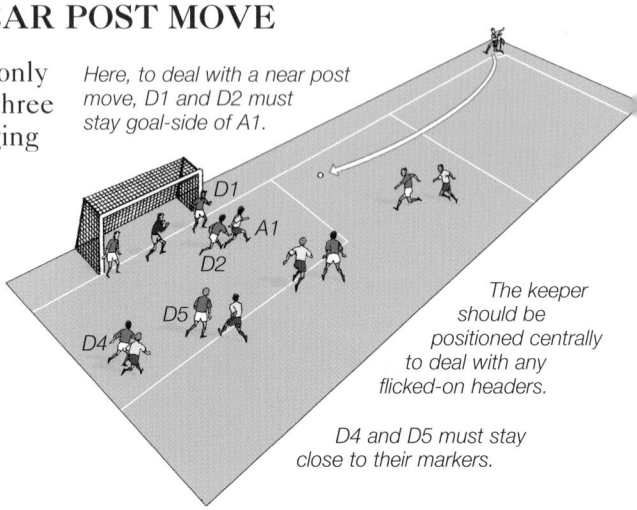

Here, to deal with a near post move, D1 and D2 must stay goal-side of A1.

The keeper should be positioned centrally to deal with any flicked-on headers.

D4 and D5 must stay close to their markers.

THE OUTSWINGER

The outswinging corner is aimed at players on the edge of the penalty area who will run in and head the ball at goal.

An outswinging cross

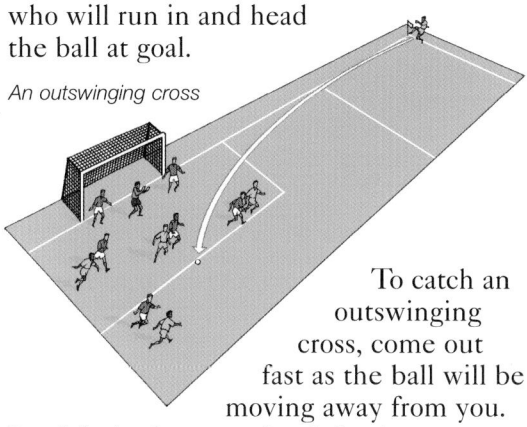

To catch an outswinging cross, come out fast as the ball will be moving away from you. It might be better to let defenders deal with it, so be ready to make a save.

THE SHORT CORNER

Short corners allow opponents to keep possession of the ball while they decide whether to cross or try a long-range shot.

A short corner

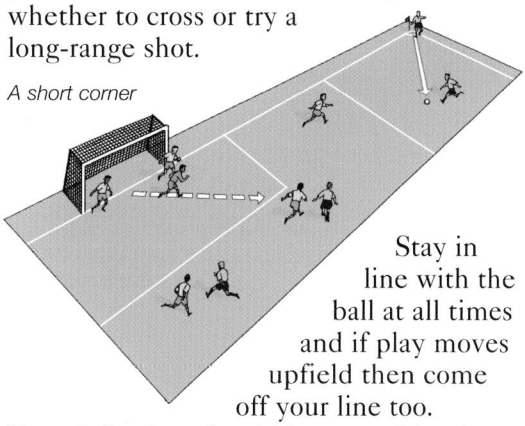

Stay in line with the ball at all times and if play moves upfield then come off your line too. Your defenders should keep marking in case of a sudden cross.

LONG THROW-INS

Long throw-ins are becoming very popular as a way of getting the ball into the goal area. Most teams will have a player who can easily throw the ball deep into the penalty area. Treat long throw-ins like near post corners, as your opponents will try to use a three touch move.

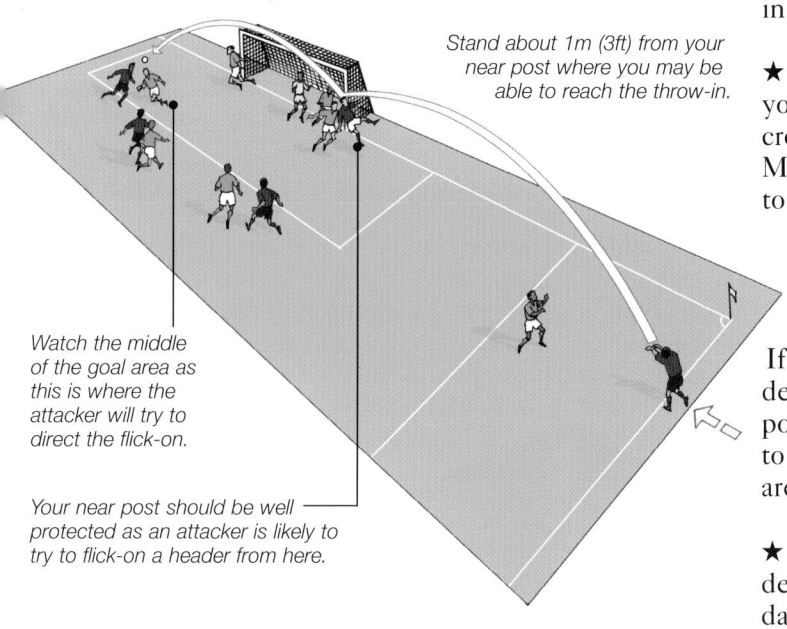

You should be able to tell when a long throw-in is about to happen. The thrower will take a long run-up before throwing and your opponents will push taller players into your penalty area.

SET PIECE TIPS

★ Stand near the middle of the goal at corners, so you can cover any part of your goal area. Watch the kicker, but be aware of movements in the penalty area.

★ Don't get blocked on your line by players crowding in front of you. Move around on your line to make some space.

★ You should treat corners in the same way as crosses (see page 16). If you think you can safely deal with the ball, then be positive and go for it. Try to take charge of your goal area and be decisive.

★ Short throw-ins in your defending third can be dangerous. Defenders should mark the attackers in and around the penalty area and you should be ready for a cross.

FREE KICKS AND PENALTIES

Penalties and direct free kicks, where the taker of the kick can shoot straight for goal, give your opponents a good scoring opportunity. You can organize defensive cover at free kicks, but penalties are a challenge for you alone. They give you the chance to pull off a great save.

CENTRAL FREE KICKS

To reduce the chances of a goal from a central direct free kick, you need to form a defensive wall. You and your team-mates should work out in practice where everyone is positioned for free kicks and who will organize the wall.

In a match, if you are organizing the wall, then you need to do it quickly before your opponents catch you out of position. The wall must be at least 9m (30ft) away from the kick. It should be lined up slightly past the near post to make swerve shots more difficult.

The wall covers the near post, and the keeper covers the far post.

To see the kicker clearly, the keeper stands well to the side of the wall.

There should be about five players in a wall. One player runs out to block a sideways pass.

The player in line with the near post must be quite tall to make chip shots harder.

If a chip or swerve shot gets past the wall, you may have time to move across and save it.

WIDE FREE KICKS

There is less chance of a shot from a wide free kick, so the wall does not need so many players in it. A two or three player wall can block a deep cross into the goal area. Stand in the centre of your goal about 2m (6ft) off your line.

A small wall allows other players to mark opponents.

KICKS INSIDE THE AREA

Indirect free kicks, where the ball has to touch another player before it enters the goal, can be awarded in the penalty area. These can occur in very dangerous positions, so bring as many players behind the ball as possible.

For central kicks, the keeper should rush out as the kick is taken.

SAVING PENALTIES

The outcome of a penalty kick can decide the result of a game, but all the pressure is on the penalty-taker, because the whole of his team will expect him to score. Before the kick is taken, move from side to side if you want to. You can't move forwards until after the ball has been kicked.

Moving from side to side along your goal-line may help distract the penalty-taker before he takes the kick.

Watch to see if the taker keeps looking at one particular side of the goal before he kicks. But don't assume he's definitely going to shoot in that direction – he may be trying to trick you. Try to delay your dive until the kick has actually been taken. Don't try to anticipate a shot – react to one.

Use any technique to save a penalty. Fall slightly forwards as you dive to put more power behind a tip and keep the ball out of the goal.

DUMMY TACTIC

A 'dummy' is a way of fooling your opponents by pretending to move in one direction but then actually going in the other. You can use, or 'sell', a dummy to try to make a penalty-taker shoot at a particular part of the goal.

1. As the taker runs up to kick, sell a dummy left or right, as if you are about to dive to this side.

2. Dive to the opposite side. The taker may be fooled into shooting where you want him to.

WATCH THE RUN-UP

Watching the penalty-taker's run-up may tell you which side of the goal he is aiming for. Straight run-ups are difficult to predict, because the kicker may choose either side or may kick straight ahead.

Angled run-up – left-footed shot goes to the left.

Angled run-ups can result in shots aimed at the same side of the goal as the kicking foot.

Curved run-up – right-footed shot goes to the left.

Curved run-ups often lead to shots into the opposite side of the goal to the kicking foot.

RECOVERY SAVE PRACTICE

In some situations, you might have to make a recovery save, where you aren't able to use correct technique but need to dive for the ball instinctively. It is difficult to learn the quick reactions needed, but regular practice will help sharpen up your reflexes.

DEFLECTED SHOTS

If a shot is fired low into a crowded penalty area, there is a chance that it may bounce off a leg or foot, and change direction. You could then be left well out of position.

To practise saving deflected shots, put a row of three heavy 1m (3ft) high markers 6m (20ft) out from goal, with a gap of 60cm (2ft) between each one. Ask a team-mate to stand 5m (16ft) further back and fire shots at goal. Some shots will deflect off the markers.

Only move after the shot has been made.

You have to react very fast to save a deflected shot. If you are wrong-footed by a deflection, try to save with your feet (see page 9).

Keep your weight well balanced and don't dive too early.

OVERHEAD LOBS

If you are caught out of position, an attacker may lob, or chip, the ball over you. As lob shots travel slowly, you have the chance to recover your position with quick footwork and make a save.

To practise this, place a marker 6m (20ft) from the centre of the goal and ask a team-mate to stand on the penalty spot with a ball. Run out and touch the marker.

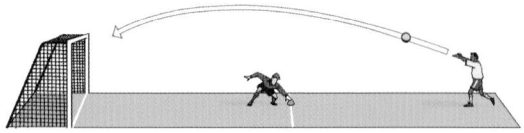

As you touch it, your team-mate throws the ball over your head. Step back quickly and leap up. Try to tip the ball over the bar (see page 11).

This game should improve your jumping technique.

As you step back, turn sideways slightly so that you are facing the ball more.

THE REFLEX SAVE

When there are many players in front of you, blocking your view of play, you might have to react very quickly to deal with a shot that you only see at the last moment. To practise reflex saves, stand in the centre of the goal with your back to a team-mate who stands about 12m (39ft) out from goal.

When your team-mate shouts 'Turn!' he shoots at goal while you turn around and try to make a save.

You will need to react fast and make a reflex, or instinctive, save.

Your team-mate shouldn't aim too far away from your body and should vary his position before each shot.

Don't worry about your technique. Catch a shot if you can, but if not, try to block or tip it. When you see a low shot very late, saving with your feet might be the best option (see page 9). Practise regularly to speed up your reflexes.

THE FOLLOW-UP SAVE

Whenever you make a save but do not keep possession of the ball, always get back into position quickly, so that you are able to deal with a follow-up shot.

This game will help you practise getting in line with the ball, making a save and then rapidly recovering your position.

This game is very tiring, so rest after each pair of saves or swap around with another keeper.

Stand in the centre of the goal and ask four team-mates, each with a ball, to position themselves an equal distance apart, 15m (49ft) out from goal. Get in line and save from the player furthest to the right. Then save from the next player along who shoots just as you complete the first save. Repeat the exercise with the players on the left.

Your coach could number each striker from 1 to 4 and then shout out one of the numbers. You then save from this player.

PRE-MATCH PREPARATION

It's important that you develop a regular routine before a game, so that you are well prepared, both physically and mentally. You should approach a game with a positive attitude, feeling fit and confident. Just before a game, make sure you do a proper warm-up and some handling practice.

PRE-MATCH TIPS

★ Try to get a good night's sleep before a game and don't do anything too energetic the day before. It's best to be well rested and alert.

★ Be careful about what you eat before a game. You need to eat well to give yourself energy, but don't eat a large meal just before exercising.

★ Spend time sorting out your kit. Take kit, such as tracksuit bottoms and a cap, which will be useful in different types of weather.

★ When you arrive at the pitch, check the quality of the playing surface and keep an eye on the weather conditions, as these might affect the game.

★ Try not to get too nervous in the build-up to a game. Getting worried and stressed wastes a lot of energy, so stay calm and relaxed.

★ Before you warm up, discuss defensive tactics with your team-mates, to make sure everyone knows what to do at set piece plays and corners.

STRETCHING AND LOOSENING EXERCISES

Warming up before a game is essential. If you don't loosen up your muscles, you could get injured. Exercise for about ten minutes until you feel warmer, but don't tire yourself out. After finishing these exercises, do some gentle jogging.

To loosen your neck muscles, gently roll your head around in a circle ten times. Then do the same the other way around. This is a very relaxing exercise.

To exercise your shoulders and arms, bend well forwards with your legs 30cm (1ft) apart. With your hands on your shoulders, roll both arms around.

To loosen your hamstring muscles, lift up one leg and bend the knee back until you can hold your ankle in your hand. Then do the same with your other leg.

BALL WORK

Getting the feel of the ball will help your handling during a game. Basic routines will improve your timing and get you focused.

Some of the exercises earlier in the book such as high and low shot practice (see page 7) would be ideal, as are the ones below.

Move the ball in a circle around your body, passing it from one hand to the other behind your back. Start at waist height and move up to chest level.

Lie on your stomach with your arms in front of you. Ask a team-mate to throw catches to you from about 2m (6ft) away. Raise your legs as you catch.

To sharpen your reflexes, ask a team-mate to stand 2m (6ft) away holding a ball at chest height. When he drops the ball, catch it before it hits the ground.

STAY FOCUSED

During a game you may not touch the ball for long periods, but stay focused at all times, or you may start making mistakes. Always use good technique and never get casual about making saves.

This keeper stopped concentrating for a moment and is now unable to get to this long-range shot.

BE CONFIDENT

As the last line of defence for your team, you need to seem confident at all times.

American keeper Kasey Keller shows his confidence by claiming a catch early on in a game.

If you appear nervous, the opposing team might think your technique is weak and could try to pressurize you. Believe in your own ability to play well and remember that you are a crucial player in your team.

INDEX

attacking third 3, 16, 21, 22

back pass 3, 22, 23
backswing 3, 20
barrier position 7

catching 5, 6, 7, 10, 16, 17
  scooping 6, 7
  W shape 5, 6, 10, 16
chip shot 13, 26, 28
collapsing save 8
communication 2, 16, 22, 24
co-ordination 2
corner 17, 23, 24, 25, 30
  near post 24
  outswinging 25
  short 25
crosses 16, 17, 19, 22, 25

defending third 3, 12, 13, 19, 24
defensive wall 26
deflected shot 28
diving at feet 14, 15
diving save 9, 10, 11
dummy tactics 27

far post 3, 16, 24, 26
follow-through 3, 18, 20
foot, parts of 3
footwork 6, 7, 11, 12, 28

free kick 20, 23, 26
  central 26
  in the area 26
  wide 26

goal area 4, 13, 16, 17, 21, 24, 25
goal kick 20, 23

inside (of foot) 3
instep 3, 20, 21

kicking 19, 20, 21, 23
  clearance kick 23
  half-volley 21
  place kick 20
  volley 20
kit 4, 30

landing 10
laws, goalkeeping 3
lob shots 13, 26, 28

middle third 3, 22

narrowing the angle 12, 13, 14, 15, 16
near post 3, 16, 24, 25, 26

offside 22, 23, 24
one-on-ones 14, 15
outfield players 23

penalties 27
penalty area 3, 4, 13, 16, 21, 22, 25, 26, 28
pitch, parts of 3, 19, 21
positioning 2, 12, 13, 14, 15, 16, 22, 24, 26, 28, 29
preparation, pre-match 30, 31
punching 16, 17

saves
  collapsing 8
  diving 9, 10, 11
  follow-up 29
  reflex 29
  spreading 15
  with feet 9, 28
scooping 6, 7
set piece plays 24, 25, 26, 30
spreading yourself 15
stance, goalkeeper's 4, 8, 10, 14
sweeper 23

throw-in 3, 23, 24, 25
throwing 16, 18, 19
tipping 11, 16, 17, 27, 28, 29

W shape catch 5, 6, 10, 16
warming up 30

If you would like to improve your soccer by attending a soccer course in your holidays, you can find out about different courses from:

Bobby Charlton International Ltd.
Hopwood Hall, Rochdale Road
Middleton, Manchester M24 6XH
Tel: 0161 643 3113

This edition first published in 2002 by Usborne Publishing Ltd., 83-85 Saffron Hill, London EC1N 8RT, England. www.usborne.com

Copyright © 1998, 2002 Usborne Publishing Ltd.

The name Usborne and the devices ⚲ ⚇ are Trade Marks of Usborne Publishing Ltd. All rights reserved. No part of this publication may be reproduced, stored in a retrieval system or transmitted in any form or by any means, electronic, mechanical, photocopying, recording or otherwise, without the prior permission of the publisher.

Printed in Belgium.